Share the Shaka

Tifney Bertram

PAGE PUBLISHING, INC.
New York, NY

First originally published by Page Publishing, Inc. 2019

ISBN 978-1-64350-800-9 (Hardcover)
ISBN 978-1-64350-799-6 (Digital)

Printed in the United States of America

For my Pop.

"Peanut Butter, Jelly Jam, Tiffy Tuff is Who I Am"

Paul's wide eyes peered out of the airplane's window onto a green land surrounded by white-capped water with blue crests. The tropical island below would soon be his new home.

As the plane made its descent toward the runway, Paul felt a sense of fear and excitement. He would be the new kid in a very different place.

Along the winding highway to his new house, he passed a bus driver, some construction workers, a fruit stand worker, a gas station attendant, and the mailman.

All of these people, with smiling faces, flashed the same wave of their hand. But this wave was different.

4

Paul and his family pulled into the driveway of their new home and Kai, the neighbor, who looked to be about the same age as Paul, came over to greet Paul.

"Hi! I'm Kai. I live next door," Kai introduced himself and waved. It was the same wave Paul had seen earlier. This must be a secret Hawaiian wave!

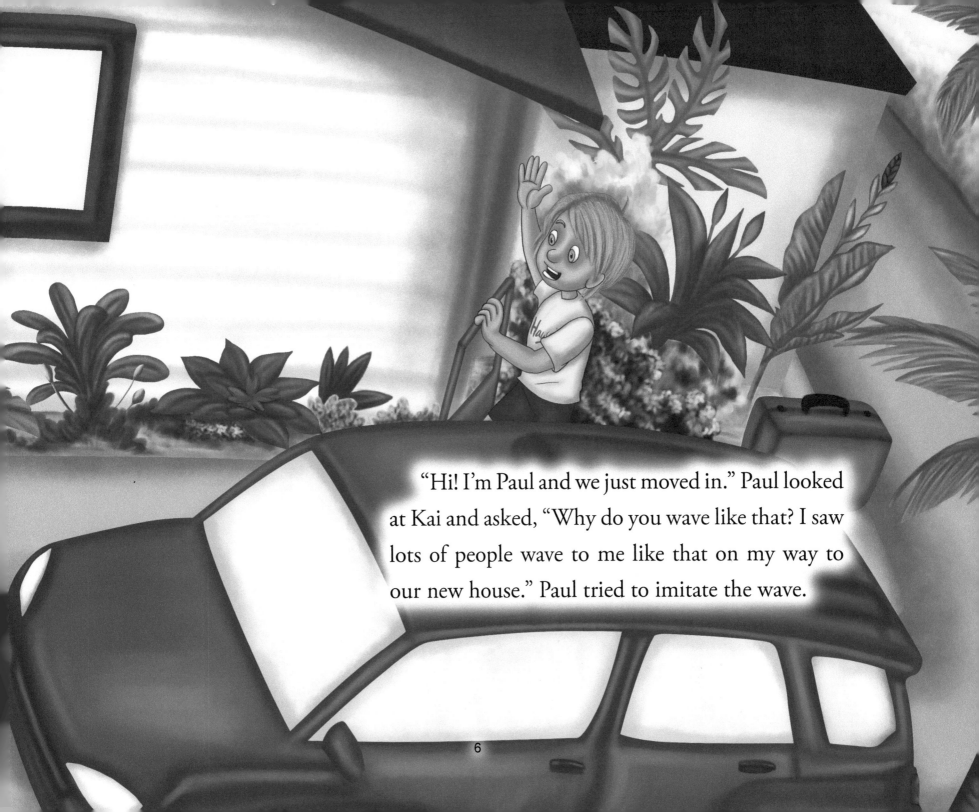

"Hi! I'm Paul and we just moved in." Paul looked at Kai and asked, "Why do you wave like that? I saw lots of people wave to me like that on my way to our new house." Paul tried to imitate the wave.

"Shaka!" Kai smiled and shouted. "This is the shaka! It is a friendly gesture that represents the aloha spirit. It means hello. It means goodbye.

It means thank you. It means see you later. It means aloha! It means a lot of things! We all share the shaka here in Hawaii."

7

"How did people start waving this 'shaka'? Where did it come from? Who started it?" Paul inquired.

"Hmmmm . . . I don't know! Let's go ask Uncle Kimo at the surf shack. He might know!" Kai was a seasoned surfer and loved to go talk story with Uncle Kimo.

8

"Aloha, Uncle! Do you know where the shaka came from? How it started?"

"Sorry, I do not know," Uncle Kimo replied. "But I do know the surf's up today! Take this surfboard and show your new friend a thing or two about surfing!"

On the way to the beach, Kai and Paul passed by Uncle Ike's ukulele shop and stopped in. Kai loved to strum on the ukulele while he watched the ocean's waves roll in.

"Aloha, Uncle! Do you know where the shaka came from? How it started?"

"Sorry, Kai, I do not know. But here is a ukulele for your new friend. Maybe you'll give him some lessons!" Uncle Ike selected a small ukulele and handed it to Paul.

"Thank you so much, sir," Paul said gratefully. These were the friendliest people Paul had ever met!

13

Kai and Paul sat under a big banyan tree on the shore. Kai strummed on the ukulele while Paul listened and watched the waves roll in. Kai told Paul that the waves were too big for Paul's first surf lesson. So Kai taught Paul a few chords on the four-stringed instrument and then they headed to Auntie Kanani's for a plate lunch.

"Aloha, Auntie! This is my new neighbor, Paul. We are trying to find out how the shaka started. Where it came from? Do you know?"

Auntie Kanani didn't know. But she did know how to cook! She served up two kalua pork plate lunches with potato and macaroni salad!

They boys gobbled up their ono lunches and then headed to Auntie Chevy's shave-ice stand for dessert.

PLATE LUNCH SPECIALS
$7.50
Laulau
Chicken Katsu
Poke
Loco Moco
Kalua Pig
BROKE DA MOUTH

16

"Aloha, Auntie! Do you know where the shaka came from? How it started?"

"Sorry, Kai. I do not know. But here is your favorite pineapple flavored shave-ice. And what flavor would you like?" Auntie Chevy asked Paul.

"Grape!" Paul shouted.

Paul and Kai meandered down the red dirt road, slurping on their shave-ices. "Let's go ask Auntie Pua at the lei stand. She might know!" Kai suggested.

"Aloha, Auntie! This is my new neighbor, Paul. He just moved to Hawaii. We are trying to find out where the shaka came from? How it started. Do you know??"

"No. Sorry, I don't know," replied Auntie Pua, "but here is a plumeria lei for your new friend! Welcome to Hawaii! Aloha!"

"Wow, thanks," Paul said as he bent his head to accept the lei.

The boys wondered where they could go next . . .

FRESH
FLOWERS
LEIS

20

"Hey! I know!" Kai exclaimed. "My tutu works at the library!"

"Your . . . uh . . . tutu??" Paul questioned.

"My grandma! In Hawaii, grandmas are called tutus. Let's go see if she knows!" Kai and Paul gathered up the surfboard, the ukulele, and finished up their shave-ices and headed for the library.

"Hi, Tutu!" Kai hugged and kissed his grandma. "This is my friend Paul. He just moved to Hawaii, and we are trying to find out how the shaka started. We have visited Uncle Kimo at the surf shack, Uncle Ike at the ukulele shop, Auntie Kanani for a plate lunch, Auntie Chevy for a shave-ice, and Auntie Pua at the lei stand. Tutu, do *you* know how the shaka started?" Kai pleaded.

"Yes! I know the legend of the shaka and how it came to be. Have a seat here and I will share the shaka story with you." The boys sat up on the library couch and listened.

"Long ago, there was a sugar mill worker on the island of O'ahu who lost these three fingers in a sugar mill accident." Kai's tutu held her three middle fingers. "This worker was unable to work in the mill any longer, but he was such a good worker, the sugar mill owner decided to make him a guard for the mill's train. Every day, the worker would wave to the passersby with his hand that was missing three fingers. The passersby would wave back with their thumb and pinkie, just like his hand. Since then, Hawaiians have waved the shaka to each other!"

Kai and Paul looked at each other. At the same time, they shouted, "Let's go share the shaka!" They ran out of the library to share what they learned with Auntie Chevy, Uncle Ike, Auntie Kanani, Uncle Kimo, and Auntie Pua.

When they returned to their homes later in the afternoon, tired and happy, Paul and Kai turned to each other and smiled. They knew they would be great friends. As they turned to go down the paths to their homes, they looked at each other and shared the shaka.

About the Author

Tifney Bertram was born and raised in Southern California. She was a middle-school math teacher for ten years before moving to Kilauea, Hawaii, in 2009. While living on Kauai, she learned to appreciate the aloha spirit. She and her husband had a fruit and flower farm. She owned a wedding floral business, and they also supplied local restaurants with fresh fruits.

In 2015, they moved to Bend, Oregon, where, surprisingly, winter became Tifney's favorite season. She owns a local nut-roasting business and participates in local outdoor markets and supplies also to small stores.

Tifney enjoys travel, snowboarding, surfing, and dogs, especially golden retrievers.

CPSIA information can be obtained
at www.ICGtesting.com
Printed in the USA
BVHW090832110319
542309BV00015B/228/P